FLOWER STREET FRIENDS

Read about the adventures of Lily Larkin and her friend, Shanta, who live on different floors of 12 Crocus Street.

Diana Hendry is a poet and the author of numerous stories for young readers, including *Harvey Angell*, Winner of the 1991 Whitbread Children's Novel Award. Among her other titles are the picture books *Dog Dottington* and *Christmas in Exeter Street*, the fiction titles *Fiona Says…*; *Sam Sticks and Delilah*; *Wonderful Robert and Sweetie-Pie Nell*; *Kid Kibble* and a novel for older children, *Minders*.

Lily lived at 12 Crocus Street,
Lumpstead, Lumfrey.

FLOWER STREET FRIENDS

Written by
DIANA HENDRY

Illustrated by
JULIE DOUGLAS

WALKER BOOKS
AND SUBSIDIARIES
LONDON • BOSTON • SYDNEY

For Charlotte Hitchcock Bard

The lines on page 76 are from "The Swing"
in *A Child's Garden of Verse*,
by Robert Louis Stevenson

First published 1995 by Walker Books Ltd
87 Vauxhall Walk, London SE11 5HJ

This edition published 1999

2 4 6 8 10 9 7 5 3 1

Text © 1995 Diana Hendry
Illustrations © 1995 Julie Douglas

This book has been typeset in Plantin Light.

Printed in England by Clays Ltd, St Ives plc

British Library Cataloguing in Publication Data
A catalogue record for this book is available
from the British Library.

ISBN 0-7445-7227-4

CONTENTS

You would know Lily Larkin if you saw her because she always wears one red sock and one yellow sock.

Red Sock, Yellow Sock

You would know Lily Larkin if you saw her, not just because she has ginger hair (that goes every which way) and round pink specs, but because she always wears one red sock and one yellow sock.

"She looks nothing like a lily," Lily's gran often said. "Lilies are tall and pale and delicate and our Lily is short and sturdy and bright." Gran always smiled when she said this, as if she much preferred the two-legged, red-and-yellow-socked Lily to the garden or field lily.

Lily lived at 12 Crocus Street, Lumpstead, Lumfrey LF1 MF2. Lily remembered her post code because her mother said it meant "Lots of Fun for 1 but More Fun for 2".

Lumpstead was a big city. It had lots of shops and offices, schools and churches, hospitals and theatres, parks and swimming pools. When Lily went out into her back-yard she could hear the strange music of Lumpstead–car-hum, bird-song, ambulance-wail and people-chatter all mixed together.

The bit of the city where Lily lived was made up of one fat street, called Flower Street, and five thin streets running off it – all named after flowers. So there was Primrose Street, Harebell Street, Daisy Street, Snowdrop Street and Crocus Street.

"Thank goodness there isn't a Lily Street," Lily's gran said, but Lily herself thought it would be wonderful to be Lily of Lily Street and wished that either whoever had named the street had thought about lilies or that Lumpstead could grow another flower street and call it Lily Street.

Number 12 Crocus Street was divided into three flats. Lily's gran lived in the bottom flat, Lily lived in the middle flat with her mother and her brother Sam and the top flat was empty because the last people to live there had just left.

Mrs Larkin said, "Now we can have some peace and quiet," because the last people had been two students who had a lot of late night parties which kept Mrs Larkin awake. But Lily missed the students and waking up in the middle of the night to music. Sometimes Lily had got out of bed and danced about her bedroom and then gone back to bed and fallen fast asleep.

Now there were no sounds at all from the flat upstairs. No music, no laughter, no *burble gurgle* of the bath running or *whush-shush* of the lavatory flush, no feet running up and down stairs, no slamming of doors and rows that made all the Larkins hold their breath with excitement.

Mrs Larkin said the student rows were like the student parties. They gave her a headache. (Mrs Larkin had a lot of headaches.) But now it was all silent in the upstairs flat and Lily thought it was lonely not having anyone above them. It was like having an empty sky, a sky without sun, rain, wind and snow in it.

Lily's gran didn't have headaches. She had sore feet. She had sore feet because she was on them a lot, she said. And she was on them a lot because she did ironing for people who didn't have time to do their own. There was a sign in Gran's front window which said MIRANDA'S IRONING SERVICES.

*Lily could hardly find Gran among the dresses and
skirts, trousers and shirts, sheets and towels. . .*

(Miranda was Gran's name.)

Sometimes, when Lily went down to visit Gran in the bottom flat, she could hardly find her among the dresses and skirts, trousers and shirts, sheets and towels that hung everywhere. And then she had to follow her ears because Gran usually sang as she ironed.

It was because of Miranda-Gran's ironing that Lily began wearing one red sock and one yellow sock. When she was ironing, Miranda-Gran was always losing tops that went with bottoms, or bottoms that went with tops. "How I hate things that match," Miranda-Gran said, searching through a great basket of clothes for a blue striped shirt that should have gone with a blue striped skirt and only finding a red striped skirt and a green striped skirt but no *blue* striped skirt.

Lily, sitting on Gran's kitchen stool and swinging her feet up and down, looked at her two white-socked feet and thought that Gran was right. Matching things were very dull and she went upstairs to her own flat and dug about in the sock drawer and found one red sock and one yellow sock and put them on. And everyone liked them very much.

Miranda-Gran said she wished they made shoes in two colours so that you could have a red left shoe and a yellow right shoe. Lily's mother said red and yellow socks didn't show the dirt nearly as much as white socks and they were very cheerful to look at on a dull morning. And Lily's brother Sam, who said as little as possible, took one look at Lily's feet and said, "Like the socks, Lill!" And this was a very big compliment.

Lily's dad, who lived three streets up in

Harebell Street, looked at the socks and smiled. On Lily's birthday he brought her six pairs of red socks and six pairs of yellow socks and mixed them together, and Lily was very pleased indeed and sometimes made her feet talk to each other because a red-socked foot has a very different character to a yellow-socked foot.

And then someone came to live in the upstairs flat who didn't believe in things matching either and Gran took one look at her and said, "She'll make the perfect friend for you, Lily Larkin."

Her name was Shanta and she had dozens of plaits. The plaits were pencil-thin and tightly bound so that they stuck out all over Shanta's head and each one was tied at the end with a brightly coloured ribbon or bobble.

Lily was sitting on the front wall when

Shanta arrived. The front door was open. Shanta rode on her father's shoulders and Mr Salkey ran up the stairs saying, "Here we go! Here we go! Here we go!" Shanta, bobbing and laughing on her father's shoulders, had to duck her head so that she didn't bang it on the ceiling. After them came Mrs Salkey with a small bundle of baby in her arms. Mrs Salkey was large and slow and she didn't speak to Lily and Lily didn't speak to Mrs Salkey but they smiled at each other.

When Mrs Salkey had gone slowly up the stairs, Lily sat very still on the wall and shut her eyes and even with her eyes shut Shanta's coloured ribbons and bobbles danced before her eyes like it was Christmas time and then she jumped off the wall and ran in to see Miranda-Gran.

"Did you see? Did you see?" Lily asked,

Shanta was sitting on her daddy's shoulders.

pushing her way through the dangling dresses and making the metal hangers rattle and chatter together.

"I did indeed," said Gran and a hiss of steam, like the sigh of a small dragon, came from the iron. "Ribbons and bobbles!" said Gran.

So then Lily ran upstairs to her own flat, where Mrs Larkin was mopping the kitchen floor while Sam sat at the kitchen table with his feet up on a chair, reading a comic. "Did you see? Did you see?" Lily cried.

"I heard people arriving," said Mrs Larkin, "and I looked out into the hall and I saw a little girl about ten feet tall with her head all covered in ribbons."

"And bobbles!" said Lily. "She had ribbons and bobbles and she wasn't ten feet tall. She was sitting on her daddy's shoulders."

"That explains it," said Mrs Larkin.

"Did you see?" Lily asked Sam, but Sam only said, "Uh-huh!" without looking up from his comic, so Lily went downstairs and outside again to sit on the wall and very soon a blue van arrived with furniture inside and Mr Salkey, wearing a large orange velvet cap, came downstairs and helped the furniture man carry things upstairs – tables and chairs and beds and cupboards and pots and pans and a pram which Mr Salkey asked Mrs Larkin if he could leave in the hall. And there was no sign of Shanta at all.

Miranda-Gran said she was probably helping her mum put things in their proper places and there were lots of bumps and bangs from upstairs which suggested that this was so.

Mrs Larkin said, "I'll ask them all down for a cup of tea later this afternoon."

"When? When?" Lily kept asking until her mother got impatient and said, "For goodness' sake, Lily, go out and play in the yard!"

"Boring!" said Lily, but she went out into the yard, banging the door crossly behind her.

At the end of the yard, in the only square of soil, grew an apple tree. And there was Shanta, jumping up and down underneath it and trying to reach an apple. When she jumped, all her ribbons and bobbles jumped too.

Lily sat on the back step and watched.

Once upon a time, Miranda-Gran had told Lily, all this part of the city had been orchards and that was why a lot of the yards and gardens still had apple trees. Lily liked to look down Crocus Street and imagine it as a big orchard full of trees.

Shanta jumped and jumped but she couldn't reach an apple.

So then Shanta sang to the apples.

"Apple, apple, drop on my head,
I'll shine you and shine you
And take you to bed!"

The song made Lily laugh.

"They're cooking apples," she said. "They make your mouth go 'ouch' unless you cook them with lots of sugar."

Then Shanta stopped jumping up and down and singing to the apple tree and came to sit beside Lily on the back step.

"I like your socks," she said.

"I like your ribbons and bobbles," said Lily.

"I've got some spare ribbons," said Shanta. "Would you like to borrow them?"

"Yes," said Lily. "And I've got some spare socks. Would you like to borrow them?"

"Yes," said Shanta.

So when, eventually, Mrs Larkin, Miranda-Gran, Sam, Mr and Mrs Salkey and baby Salkey were all having a cup of tea in the middle flat, two little girls appeared with red and yellow socks and lots of ribbons and bobbles in their hair and Miranda-Gran laughed and said, "I knew you'd be friends."

Miranda-Gran was trying to plait Lily's hair.

LF1 MF2

It was Sunday night. Sam was flopped on the sofa, watching television. Miranda-Gran was trying to plait Lily's hair. Mrs Larkin was washing up.

"Tomorrow morning," she said, "I think it would be very nice, Sam, if you showed Mrs Salkey and Shanta the neighbourhood."

"Uh-huh!" said Sam. And then he jerked upright like a puppet hauled out of his box by his strings, and said, "Who? Me? You must be joking!"

"I am not joking," said Mrs Larkin. "Mrs Salkey needs to know where the baker's is and the post office and the health centre."

"And the nursery school and the park," said Miranda-Gran.

"Yes," said Mrs Larkin. "Those too."

"Why can't you do it?" asked Sam.

"Because I'm working," said Mrs Larkin. "Mondays and Wednesdays and Fridays, remember? At the baker's. And you've got a whole week's holiday before you go back to school."

Sam fell back on the sofa. "Oh, stress! Stress!" he said, hitting his forehead with his hand.

"He's shy," Miranda-Gran explained to Lily and Lily thought shyness must be like a very bad tummy ache because it made Sam curl up on the sofa as if he were a snail going into his shell.

"Can I go too?" asked Lily. "I can show Shanta the cats and the lamppost with a hat on."

Sam put a pillow over his head and groaned.

"What a good idea," said Mrs Larkin.

"And I could meet you all for lunch at the café," said Miranda-Gran. Lily bounced up and down so much at this that all Gran's careful plaits came undone.

"I'll go upstairs now and invite them," said Mrs Larkin.

"Maya says she would appreciate your help," Mrs Larkin reported when she came downstairs again. (Maya was Mrs Salkey. Lily liked the way their names went together – Maya and Shanta.)

So Monday morning found Mrs Salkey (with the baby, Winston, on her back), Shanta, Sam and Lily all going down Crocus Street together – well, maybe not quite together because Shanta and Lily hopped and skipped and bumped each other and

Mrs Salkey swung along in a slow and happy way so that baby Winston, resting his cheek on her back, fell fast asleep. Sam looked red-faced and shy and tried to pretend he was all by himself. But soon he seemed to feel better because Mrs Salkey was very un-shy and because she didn't ask him any of the questions he hated, like "How is school?" and "How old are you?" (Sam hated these questions because school was awful and he was twelve and wanted to be fourteen.)

As they walked up Crocus Street, Lily introduced Shanta to the cats. There were a lot of cats in Crocus Street and they liked to sit on the windowsills of their houses. Lily knew most of them by name.

"This one's Muggins, and this one's Hercules," she told Shanta. (Hercules was a very large orange cat.) "And this one is Tabitha and this one's Harry!"

And Shanta shook paws with those cats willing to have their paws shaken and said, "Hello, Mr Muggins. Hello, Mr Hercules," and so on, until Sam said, "If we stop to say hello to *every* cat we meet we'll never get anywhere!" And Mrs Salkey said, "Oh well, we're not in a hurry."

At the top of Crocus Street they turned left into Snowdrop Street.

"My nose tells me where we're going," said Mrs Salkey. "We're going to the baker's." And she was right.

Lily liked the baker's. Mr Herbert ran the baker's shop and it wasn't so much a shop as a big shed with a glass roof and metal rafters. The city pigeons liked the baker's too and sometimes one of them would fly in and perch on a rafter. Then all the women in their long white aprons (including Mrs Larkin) had to shoo it out. There were big silver shining bread ovens at the back of the baker's and tall trolleys for the baked loaves.

There were long, thin French sticks that people carried home under their arms, and white plaited loaves and big fat brown loaves. On the counter there were slices of pizza glistening with cheese and trays of cakes, and pastries – sticky lardy cakes with lots of currants buried like treasure inside them, bramble tarts, gingerbread men and Lily's favourite: doughnuts with chocolate icing. And there was a special machine for slicing bread quicker than you could say "Lily Larkin" or "Shanta Salkey".

Mrs Salkey said she'd like a brown loaf please and Mrs Larkin found one that was fresh from the oven and wrapped it up in tissue paper. "Warm as a baby," said Mrs Salkey. Mrs Larkin said she'd treat them all to a chocolate doughnut and would bring

On the counter there were trays of cakes and pastries.

them home with her that afternoon.

Next they went to the health centre. The health centre was in a square between Harebell Street and Primrose Street. Next to it was a pub, called The New England, which had chairs and tables set outside for when it was sunny. Miranda-Gran said it was good having a health centre next to the pub because both were places that could make you feel better, only in different ways.

Mrs Salkey said, yes, but the pub could make you feel a lot worse if you drank too much and stayed there too long and Miranda-Gran said *she* felt a lot worse if she stayed at the health centre too long.

To the left of the health centre was a wall with purple buddleia, like a tangle of purple curls, falling over it and a group of Crust Punks with dogs on strings, sitting beside it.

Sam took them all inside the health centre

and they looked at the photographs of the doctors and nurses pinned on the wall. There were a great many people waiting to see the doctors and a great many children bouncing on mattresses in the play room and not looking at all ill.

"Are there always so many people?" asked Mrs Salkey. And Sam said no, only on Mondays because people seemed to be iller on Mondays than on any other day of the week.

Mrs Salkey saw a notice that said there was a baby clinic every Wednesday afternoon. "Good," she said. "That's where I shall bring Winston to have him weighed." Winston woke up at that and started to cry. Mrs Salkey jiggled him up and down and Lily and Shanta pulled clown faces for him until he fell asleep again.

One of the doctors came out of his surgery

31

and looked at Lily and Shanta pulling faces for the baby. "Great socks!" he said, because they were still wearing one red and one yellow sock each. Then Lily and Shanta got the giggles and hid behind Mrs Salkey and Sam went very red and told them not to be silly.

"He's shy," Lily explained to Shanta.

"I am not!" said Sam, going redder.

"Shyness is an ag-on-y," said Mrs Salkey and that made Lily and Shanta laugh even more and dance up the street singing "Ag-on-y! Ag-on-y" until Sam said that if they didn't shut up he'd take them straight home.

The post office was easy because that was in Flower Street. Mrs Salkey said the post office was very important because she liked to write letters to her sister in Jamaica and she liked to read the cards in the post office window that offered lessons in French and beds for sale and gardeners to do your garden and plumbers to mend your taps.

After that there was just the nursery school and the park left and Sam said they wouldn't have time for the park today because they'd promised to meet Miranda-Gran in the café in Daisy Street.

"I go to nursery school three times a week," Lily told Shanta.

"I don't want to go to nursery school," said Shanta and she looked very cross.

"I think it's a good idea," said Mrs Salkey. "You could go together."

"Don't want to go!" said Shanta and she stamped first her red-socked foot and then her yellow-socked foot.

"Here it is," said Lily. "It's got pictures of us in the window. Last term we all had to draw a picture of ourselves. Look! There's me!" And Lily pointed to her own picture which had orange wool for hair, a blue crayoned dress and rice crispies stuck on as buttons.

But Shanta wouldn't look and Lily saw that she was crying. This made Lily want to cry too. Then she thought of something to cheer Shanta up and she ran ahead calling, "Come on, Shanta, I've got something to show you!" And Shanta, very curious, stopped crying and ran after her.

It was the lamppost with a hat on! It wasn't a proper lamppost any more. It was the bottom half of a knobbly old one that the council hadn't taken away when they put in new street lights. Someone had popped a red pointed traffic cone on top of the lamppost's head, just like a hat.

The lamppost with a hat on made Shanta laugh again and by then they had reached the corner café where Miranda-Gran was waiting for them.

"Lunch is on me," said Miranda-Gran. "How does pancakes followed by banana split sound?"

And all of them (apart from baby Winston, who was dreaming milky dreams) thought that pancakes and banana split sounded very nice indeed.

"Our postal code is quite right," said Lily as she and Shanta raced each other home. "There's Lots of Fun for 1 in Crocus Street, but More Fun for 2."

Next door to Lily's house lived old Mrs Melly.
Mrs Melly was nearly ninety.

A Digging Day

Next door to Lily's house lived old Mrs Melly.

Mrs Melly was nearly ninety. She was very wrinkled and bent and her house was wrinkled and bent too, because nobody had painted it for ages and Mrs Melly was too old to look after it herself.

Mrs Melly's daughter came to do the shopping for her and the Meals-on-Wheels ladies brought her lunch and everyone said that Mrs Melly would be much better living in an old people's home where she could be properly looked after. Everyone except Mrs Melly.

Mrs Melly said she was not going to move anywhere. She had lived in that house since she was a very little girl and even though there was no central heating and no bath, and an awful lot of stairs, all the things she loved most were there.

"All my memories are here," Mrs Melly told Mrs Larkin and Lily over the garden wall, "and they are the most important things of all."

So although Mrs Melly was wrinkled and bent and didn't look at all strong, she knew her own mind and it was a very strong mind.

"I'm staying put in Crocus Street," said Mrs Melly. And she did.

But one spring day Mrs Larkin looked out of the back window and said, "Oh dear, poor Mrs Melly."

So Lily and Shanta looked out of the back window to see what was the matter with Mrs

Melly but Mrs Melly wasn't there at all, so Lily said, "Why is she poor Mrs Melly?"

"Well, look at her garden," said Mrs Larkin. "It used to be such a pretty garden with lots of rosebushes and forget-me-nots and irises and lupins. And now it's all weeds."

So Lily looked again, but more carefully this time. There were the beginnings of bluebells in Mrs Melly's garden, but even the bluebells couldn't grow very well because of the weeds. The weeds spread over Mrs Melly's garden like a piece of knitting that went on and on and on. Over the beds, down the path, round and round the rosebushes went the knitting of weeds.

"Mrs Melly's too old to look after her garden now," said Mrs Larkin. "But it's a great pity it looks like this because when she sits by her window all she can see is weeds."

"I don't know if I like Mrs Melly," said Lily. "She glares at me."

"That's because she can't see very well," said Mrs Larkin. "She's lived in that house since she was a little girl just like you, Lily. It must make her sad to see it looking like this."

So then Lily looked at Mrs Melly's garden and Mrs Melly's house and tried to unbend and unwrinkle Mrs Melly and imagine her as a little girl, but it was very hard.

"Perhaps we could do her garden for her?" said Shanta. "And make it all nice again."

"Perhaps," said Mrs Larkin. "But Mrs Melly is quite a difficult old lady. She doesn't like people doing her favours."

"What's a favour?" asked Lily.

"Well, it's someone doing something kind for you without asking anything in return," said her mother.

"Like someone giving you a present when you haven't got one for them," said Shanta.

"That's it exactly," said Mrs Larkin.

"We'll have to ask her for a favour," said Shanta, "and then it will be fair."

"We could ask for a memory," said Lily.

Then Mrs Larkin looked very surprised and said, "Now *that's* a very good idea!"

So Mrs Larkin told Miranda-Gran and Sam about Lily's idea of doing Mrs Melly's garden in exchange for a memory, and Miranda-Gran thought for a long time and then she said, "Yes, that would be two kinds of digging – digging to find memories and digging to dig up weeds."

And Sam said, "Not bad, our Lill!" (Which meant, very good indeed!)

Shanta told her mum and dad about Mrs Melly's garden. Mrs Salkey was very excited about it because at the back of the flats there was only the yard with the apple tree and a few pots of geraniums. So Mrs Salkey said, "Digging! And getting dirty! And growing things!"

And Mr Salkey said, "Shanta, my honeybee, have you ever seen your pop digging?"

Shanta said she never had.

"I'm a whizz!" said Mr Salkey and he tipped his orange cap on to the back of his head and laughed. "When do we start?"

Shanta said they had to ask Mrs Melly first.

Shanta told Winston about their gardening plans and Winston smiled and waved his arms in the air as if he, too, thought it was a good idea.

When it was agreed that *everyone* wanted to help, they decided that Mr Salkey, Lily and Shanta should go next door and ask Mrs Melly if they could do her garden for her in return for a memory.

Mrs Melly opened her door a crack and Mr Salkey called out, "Good morning to you, Mrs Melly, I'm from next door."

Mrs Melly opened her door a bit wider and unbent just enough to peer up at Mr Salkey, and glare. Or it looked like a glare, at first, but Lily could see that Mrs Melly was squinting her eyes behind her spectacles as if she was trying to see Mr Salkey properly.

"What d'you want?" she asked.

"Just a chat about your garden," said Mr Salkey.

"I'm too old to look after it," said Mrs Melly, crossly.

"That's what we thought," said Mr Salkey. "So we wondered if we could help."

"I don't want any help, thank you," snapped Mrs Melly and she was about to shut the door on them, when Shanta cried,

"But we want to dig and get all dirty and grow things!"

And Lily said, "And we won't do it for nothing. It's not a favour!"

Mrs Melly looked at Lily then and she said, "Oh, so you want something for it, do you, young lady?"

"Yes," said Lily. "We want a memory."

"A memory of when you were a little girl," added Shanta.

All of a sudden the wrinkles that curled downwards on Mrs Melly's face started to curl upwards as she began to laugh.

"Well, well, well! So that's your price, is it? A memory. You'd better come in."

So in they went to Mrs Melly's front room and you could see at once that it was full of memories because all of the furniture was very old and there was a big black fireplace and there were photographs of long-ago people in strange clothes all over the walls.

When Mr Salkey had sunk so deep into an old armchair that he looked as if he'd never get out again, and Lily and Shanta were perched up high on two chairs by the table, they began talking about gardens.

"Seems there's more weeds than flowers in your garden," said Mr Salkey. "Seems like you need someone just to do a little digging and weeding for you."

"And some planting," said Shanta. "The shop down the road has got packets and packets of seeds."

"It used to be a lovely garden," said Mrs Melly. "When my husband was alive he grew beautiful roses. But I can't do it now. It makes me dizzy to bend down."

"We're very good at bending down," said Lily.

"It makes me cross that I can't," said Mrs

Melly. "And I don't like taking help off folks."

"We've already told you," said Mr Salkey, "we're not doing your garden for free." He got up and looked out of the window. "I'd say doing that garden for you would cost you at least three memories."

"Of when you were little," said Shanta.

"Like us," said Lily.

"When I was a little girl there was no electric light in this house," said Mrs Melly. "We had gas lamps downstairs and to find your way to bed you had to carry a candle upstairs with you."

Lily and Shanta looked very surprised and tried to imagine what it would be like not to have electric lights and electric fires and switches to turn things off and on and Lily thought it would be very difficult to read in bed at night.

"Well, that's the first memory," said Mr Salkey. "I think we've got a deal. Can we come and garden on Saturday?"

Mrs Melly laughed and said yes, they could, and that she would have two more memories ready for them by Saturday.

On Saturday, they all put on their oldest clothes and climbed over the wall into Mrs Melly's garden. Mrs Larkin had found a small gardening fork and a trowel. Mrs Melly had her back door open and had put out a big fork and spade. So they all set to. Lily and Shanta dug up the knitting of weeds that was going round and round the rosebushes. Mrs Larkin, Miranda-Gran, and Mrs Salkey dug over the beds so that the earth looked all fresh and crumbly and the rosebushes and bluebells looked much happier. Sam sat on the wall and pointed out the weeds the others had missed.

Lily and Shanta dug up the knitting of weeds going round the rosebushes.

Mr Salkey's job was to collect all the rubbish and weeds together at the bottom of the garden and make a bonfire, which he did at lunch-time. Miranda-Gran produced some baked potatoes and sausages and they all stopped work and sat in the garden to eat, including Mrs Melly, who sat on a chair by her back door step.

"I've got my second memory ready," she said, so they gathered round to listen.

"I remember my best friend when I was eight," said Mrs Melly, "and his name was Arthur Osmund. Quite often we had to look after his baby sister and we'd walk round and round the park and sit on a seat and pretend to be mother and father. One day Arthur Osmund gave me a bag of broken biscuits and a flower."

Lily and Shanta thought this was a very nice memory.

After lunch, when all the digging was done and the beds were clear of weeds and the bonfire was burning very low, Miranda-Gran produced two packets of seeds. There was one packet of nasturtium seeds for Lily and a packet of cornflower seeds for Shanta.

Miranda-Gran showed them how to make a shallow trough for the seeds and how to drop them in carefully, so they wouldn't be too crowded when they grew into flowers. Then they covered the seeds over with the nice crumbly earth and watered them.

"It's going to be a lovely garden again," said Mrs Melly. "Would you like your third memory now?"

"Yes, please!" said Lily and Shanta.

"I'll just go and get it," said Mrs Melly, and went into her house. When she came back she was carrying a very old hoop and stick.

"Here you are," she said. "This was my favourite toy when I was a little girl. Now you two can have it. You can make the hoop roll along by beating it with a stick, or you can twizzle the hoop round your waist. If I wasn't so old I'd show you!"

Lily and Shanta said, "Thank you very much indeed" to Mrs Melly and they took the hoop and stick into their own backyard and spent the afternoon making the hoop run down the path, and after that they tried spinning it round their waists.

They had a lot of fun and both of them thought that Mrs Melly's hoop was the best memory of all.

*It was summer and Sam was busy with
the Car Wash Gang.*

THE CAR WASH GANG

It was summer and Sam was busy with the Car Wash Gang. There were four of them in the gang – Sam, Natty Liddle, Mandy Turner and Henry Chung. Sometimes the Car Wash Gang worked on summer evenings and sometimes they worked at weekends. They had buckets and sponges and bubbly liquid and cloths and they worked in pairs. Sam and Natty would go up one side of the street with a red bucket, and Mandy and Henry would go up the other side of the street with a yellow bucket.

There was nothing Lily and Shanta wanted more than to join the Car Wash Gang.

They watched Sam, Natty, Mandy and Henry getting their buckets and sponges ready. They watched, from the window, as the four went down the road knocking on doors. Some days nobody seemed to want their car washed and some days everybody seemed to want their car washed.

Lily and Shanta watched as the Gang set to work, sploshing bubbly water over the cars, rubbing and polishing, shining the windscreens, rinsing the bubbles off with clean water, cleaning the number plates. They watched as Sam, Natty, Mandy and Henry all got wetter and wetter themselves until you weren't quite sure whether they were washing cars or each other. And Lily and Shanta watched as the Gang collected the money they were paid for car washing and dropped it in a tin with a slit in the lid and a string for a handle. Afterwards the

The Gang set to work, sploshing bubbly water
over the cars.

Gang shared out the money and used it for all the extras that pocket money wouldn't stretch to – birthday presents or magazines or a new T-shirt.

"Can we join the Car Wash Gang?" Lily asked Sam almost every day and almost every day Sam said, "You're too little."

"I'm good at washing," Lily said. "Yesterday I washed the sink and the draining board."

"And I'm very strong," said Shanta. "I can carry my mum's shopping bag. I could carry the buckets of water."

"Buckets of water are *much* heavier that shopping bags. And sloppier," said Sam.

"I like slopping water," said Shanta. "I slop it in my bath."

"But you're not *meant* to slop it," said Sam. "You're meant to wash cars with it. Anyway, you two couldn't even reach the top of the car. A car with a dirty roof and clean sides would look pretty silly, wouldn't it?"

"We could do the wheels," said Lily.

"And the number plates," said Shanta.

"Oh, lay off!" said Sam. "You two stress me out." And whatever Lily and Shanta said after that, Sam wouldn't answer, so they went and washed all their dolls in the bath.

But one Sunday morning Lily heard Sam calling her.

"Put some old clothes on," said Sam, "and tell Shanta to do the same."

"Why?" asked Lily.

"You're car washing," said Sam. "Natty's ill and Mandy's gone away for the weekend."

Lily jumped up and down and then ran upstairs and banged on Shanta's door. "Put your old clothes on," she said. "We're car washing."

Both girls found their oldest T-shirts and shorts and hurried to join Sam.

"Shanta can work with me and Lily can work with Henry," said Sam. Lily and Shanta looked at each other. They wanted to stay together. "No, you can't," said Sam, reading their faces. "You'll just get silly."

So off they went, Shanta and Sam down the side of Crocus Street with even numbers on the houses, and Henry and Lily down the side of the street with odd numbers.

"I bet the odd numbers are better than the evens," said Lily. "I bet there's more people wanting their cars washed on our side."

Henry just grunted.

At the first three houses they had no luck at all.

"You could wash my car if I had one," said the man at the first house.

"Not today, thank you," said the woman at

the second house before they had a chance to ask her if she wanted her car washed.

"Haven't got any money. Sorry!" said the woman at the third house.

But at the fourth house there was a bright red (and nicely dirty) sports car outside the front door and when they knocked, a young man in pyjama trousers and bare feet came to the door.

"Like your car washed?" Henry chirped and Lily hopped from foot to foot hoping he'd say yes. The young man looked at Henry and Lily and he looked at his sports car.

"It's very dirty," said Lily. "I think it needs washing and ironing." Henry blushed when Lily said that and gave her a shove so that Lily dropped the sponges and bubbly stuff, but the young man laughed and said he thought Lily was right, only they could forget the ironing, and what did they charge?

"A pound," said Henry promptly.

"You better do a good job for that," said the young man.

"Oh, we will," said Lily. "I'm going to do the wheels and the number plates." Henry gave her another shove.

"Can you fill our bucket with warm water?" he asked and the young man went off into the house. Lily couldn't keep still she was so eager to begin.

"You got ants in your pants or something?" asked Henry. And Lily said no, she had cleaning bubbles fizzing her legs. Henry grunted again.

Then the young man brought the water and told them to knock on the door when they had finished and Lily and Henry set to work.

Henry said this was just the sort of car he

was going to have when he left school and he washed the car as carefully and tenderly as Mrs Salkey washed Winston.

Practice had made Henry a lot quicker than Lily, but she cleaned all the dirt out of the number plates at the back and front of the car, and made the rims of the wheels look nice and shiny.

"I'll do its eyes now," said Lily.

"Headlamps, you wally," said Henry but he couldn't help laughing.

The bucket of water was soon a muddy brown colour and they poured it down a drain in the road and Lily was pleased that her feet got wet at the same time because that made her a Proper Car Washer. They had to get a fresh bucket of water from the young man to wash all the bubbles off and then they polished the car with dry cloths until it looked brand new.

*Lily polished the car with dry cloths
until it looked brand new.*

"That looks great," said the young man and he gave the pound coin to Lily and it made a nice clank in her tin.

They washed two more cars after that, one a little blue mini that looked as if it had been driving through a very muddy field. (Lily was pleased with the mini because she could *almost* reach the top of it.) Henry said that the next car was a Beetle. Lily was about to tell Henry that *he* was the wally this time, but changed her mind, because she could see the shape of the car did look very like a beetle. This one was an orange beetle.

"If this is a beetle," said Lily, "the mini could be an ant."

"Dumb!" said Henry, and this time Lily felt very huffy and refused to talk to Henry any more and accidentally on purpose squeezed her sponge just where Henry's foot happened to be.

Across the road they could see that Sam and Shanta were washing a very special car indeed. It didn't look like a beetle or an ant, it looked more like a zebra because its owner had painted stripes all over it.

Shanta had made up a song about it and she sang it over and over again!

"Zebra car on a zebra crossing,
This zebra car likes a washing."

Lily and Henry helped Sam and Shanta dry the zebra car and then they compared money tins. Sam and Shanta had two pounds in their tin and Lily and Henry had three pounds in their tin.

"One more car," said Shanta, and before anyone could stop her she ran up the road and knocked on the door of number 22 Crocus Street.

"Oh, stress!" said Sam. "That's Lonika's house. She's nuts!"

But Lonika was very pleased to see Shanta. Lonika was an old lady with grey flowing hair and a lot of freckles. She came from Hungary and although she had lived in Lumpstead a long time, she was still homesick for Hungary. Everyone in Crocus Street knew that number 22 was Lonika's house because she had painted her name, in white paint, on the front door step.

"Like your car washed?" Shanta chanted just as she had heard Sam ask.

"I no have a car!" said Lonika. "I no have a husband! I no have nobody! I am Lonika – see!" And she pointed down to her name on the doorstep.

"I can't read yet," said Shanta. Sam, Henry and Lily had followed Shanta up the road and stood at the gate of Lonika's house.

"You are a very beautiful girl," Lonika told Shanta. "All your ribbons and what-you-call-'ems."

"Bobbles," said Shanta.

Lonika thought bobbles a very funny word and she tried it out several times. "Bobbles! Bobbles! Bobbles! Like things in bath, no?"

Then they all laughed and Shanta said, "Sort of. The things in the bath are bubbles."

Lonika was very pleased that she had made them all laugh. She opened her arms wide and said, "I am lonely no more! We talk and we laugh together and I no lonely. You all come in my garden and we drink together."

"Oh, stress," Sam whispered to Henry.

But Lonika went inside and found a bottle of lemonade and they all discovered they were thirsty. When the bottle was finished,

Lonika clapped them as if they were actors in a play and had played their parts very well.

"Next time you wash the cars, you come and see me?"

And even Henry said yes.

"Are we part of the Car Wash Gang now?" Lily asked Sam on the way home."

"Well ..." said Sam, "sometimes."

*Lily's dad ran down the stairs and they had
a big hug halfway.*

A SPECIALLY ORDINARY DAY

Sometimes Sam and Lily went to stay with their dad together, and sometimes Sam went by himself, and sometimes Lily went by herself.

Lily liked going alone because that way she had her dad all to herself. When Sam was there they played football together and although Lily liked this she wasn't very good at it. Or they watched television programmes that Lily found boring.

This weekend was a Lily-Only weekend and Lily was very pleased about that. Miranda-Gran took her down Snowdrop Street, left into Flower Street and left again down Harebell Street, because this was the quickest way.

Lily's dad had a room at the top of number 86 Harebell Street. Miranda-Gran didn't knock at the door, she called up to the top window. "Jack! Jack!" And Lily's dad poked his head out of the window and dropped the front door key down to them. Lily caught it because she'd practised and practised doing this.

Then Miranda-Gran opened the front door and Lily ran up the stairs and Lily's dad ran down the stairs and they had a big hug halfway. Miranda-Gran came halfway up the stairs too and said, "Hello, Jack" and Lily's dad said, "Hello, Ma. How's tricks?" And Miranda-Gran laughed and said if by "tricks" he meant the ironing business, then tricks were all right.

"I'll bring Lily back tomorrow night,"

said her dad.

"Be a good girl then, Lily," said Miranda-Gran as she *always* said. And Lily said, "All right, Gran!" which is what *she* always said, even when she wasn't planning to be good.

Miranda-Gran went back to Crocus Street then, and Lily and her dad climbed to the top of the house.

Lily's dad's flat was very tiny. It had one bed-sitting room and a tiny kitchen and a slightly larger bathroom. Lily liked it because it felt very snug and because when you looked out of the window you could see all the roofs and chimney pots making funny shapes against the sky.

There was only one bed in the room, but Lily's dad had another – a folding bed which he kept for when Lily or Sam came to stay. When they both came, he borrowed a mattress from the woman downstairs and

Sam slept on that and Lily had the folding bed.

They unfolded the folding bed now and Lily's dad fetched a duvet and pillow and Lily put Looby-Loo on the bed because then she felt properly at home in Dad's house.

"We're going to do something very special this weekend," said Lily's dad.

Lily sighed. Her dad was always trying to do something special when she came to stay. Something special often meant a long, long drive in the car. Or yet another visit to a castle – at the last count they had been to twenty-two. Or a long, long walk that wore Lily's legs out.

So Lily said, "Can't we do something ordinary this weekend?"

Lily's dad looked very surprised.

"You don't want to go to a castle?"

Lily put Looby-Loo on the bed.

Lily shook her head.

"Or out to the country for a walk?"

Lily shook her head again.

"The museum?"

"Nope!"

Lily's dad scratched his head. "Well, what *do* you want to do? What's an ordinary weekend?"

"Well," said Lily, bouncing on the folding bed so that it nearly folded up and squashed her, "we could have breakfast for a start."

"Haven't you had breakfast?"

"Two breakfasts would be sort of ordinary special," said Lily, "because we don't have breakfast together very often."

"That's true," said her dad. "And what after that?"

"I'd like to go to the park," said Lily.

"But you're *always* going to the park," said her dad.

"I know," said Lily. "But not with you. And I need someone to push me on the swing."

"Right," said her dad. "Now, I think that's a very good idea because if there is one thing that I've got a real talent for it's pushing people on swings!"

"And we could have an ice-cream," said Lily.

"We could," said her dad.

"And this afternoon you could tell me a story," said Lily.

"Oh yes, I've got a new one," said her dad. "But you've forgotten lunch. Would a pizza from the baker's be ordinary enough?"

"Yes," said Lily. "And tonight we could have a chippie."

"You mean I don't have to cook?"

"No," said Lily.

"Wonderful!" said her dad.

"And then we can snuggle up and watch television and I can stay up late!" said Lily.

"This is certainly a master plan," said her dad. "We'd better begin with breakfast."

So they did. Lily's dad made a great tower of toast. He couldn't find any marmalade so they had jam instead and Lily had a mug of milk and her dad had coffee.

"Do you think you'll be able to swing after that lot?" asked her dad. "I'm not sure I can move."

Lily said she was quite sure she could swing on the swing and dragged her dad to his feet and off they went to the park.

Lily went straight to the swings and her dad pushed. While he pushed he sang:

"How do you like to go up in a swing,
Up in the air so blue?
Oh, I do think it the pleasantest thing
Ever a child can do!"

Lily went sailing up in the air. Her feet seemed to be on a level with the top of the trees.

And when he came to the rhyming words – "swing" and "thing" and "blue" and "do" – he gave the swing an extra-big push so that Lily went sailing up in the air. Her feet seemed to be on a level with the top of the trees and she gripped very tight to the chains of the swing.

After that, Lily's dad showed her how, if she bent her legs back and then stuck them straight out in front of her, she could help to make the swing go for herself. This was good, but not nearly as good as being pushed and sung to.

When Lily's dad said he didn't have a push left in him they went and collected some conkers.

"I know lots of good games you can play with conkers," said Lily's dad.

There were plenty of conkers that had fallen on the ground. They were brown and shiny as if someone had polished them and Lily's dad filled his jacket pockets with them. Lily's pockets were rather small but she did her best so that very soon her anorak bulged at the corners like two fat cheeks.

Just as they were leaving the park they heard the jingle of the ice-cream van.

"You can't!" said Lily's dad. "Not after all that toast!"

But Lily said she just *might* be able to manage a little cornet particularly if it had a chocolate flake in it. So that's what she had.

When they got back to Harebell Street, Lily's dad found some string and some nails and showed Lily the conker game. He held one conker on a string and Lily had to try and hit his conker with her conker. But Lily kept missing and her dad said it took a lot of practice and perhaps she could ask Sam.

Instead of the conker game, Lily's dad

made some furniture. He made a doll's-house table out of one big conker and four pins and then four chairs (out of smaller conkers) to go with the table.

Then it was time to go to the baker's. So they went down Harebell Street, turned right into Flower Street and right again into Snowdrop Street.

Because it was Saturday and lunch-time, there was a long queue at the baker's. But Lily didn't mind this because there were lots of people she knew waiting in the queue.

First of all she saw Mrs Moon, her nursery school teacher, and Lily said, "Hello, Mrs Moon. This is my dad."

Mrs Moon said, "Hello, Mr Larkin, I'm very pleased to meet you."

Then Lily saw the twins, Margarita and Timian, and she said, "Hello, hello," (twice, like that, so they had one hello each).

"I'm with my dad, today," said Lily, and the twins looked up at Mr Larkin and said, "Hello, Lily's dad."

Lily's dad said hello back, but only once because he was feeling a bit shy.

At last it was their turn and Mr Larkin bought two slices of pizza and a long stick of French bread and he carried the pizza (because it was a bit sticky) and Lily carried the stick of French bread under her arm.

After lunch it was time for a story. Lily's dad made up a lot of dragon stories. There were happy dragons and sad dragons and dragons who loved singing. There were vegetarian dragons and dragons who could fly and jelly-and-ice-cream dragons.

"What sort of dragon is it today?" asked Lily.

Lily's dad settled himself down on the sofa and Lily curled up beside him.

"Today's dragon story," said Lily's dad, "is about a dragon who liked swinging on the swings in the park."

When the story was finished, Lily said, "That was the best dragon story ever!"

"You say that every time," said Lily's dad.

"It's always true," said Lily.

When it got dark, Lily and her dad went down to the chip shop (which was next to the post office in Flower Street) and they bought fish cake and chips for Lily and chicken pie and chips for Lily's dad, with lots of salt and vinegar on both of them. Then they ran back to Harebell Street before the chips could get cold and Lily's dad emptied the packets on to plates and put the plates on trays and they had their supper watching television.

After supper they cuddled up together on the sofa and Lily stayed up until half-past nine, which was very late indeed. Then Lily's dad tucked her up in the folding bed with Looby-Loo tucked in beside her.

"Was that a good sort of ordinary day?" asked Lily's dad.

"It was a very special ordinary day," said Lily.

After a while, Shanta and Lily could both go by themselves.

CHRISTMAS DAY IN CROCUS STREET

It was Christmas Eve and everyone in number 12 Crocus Street had a different idea of what they wanted to do on Christmas Day.

Miranda-Gran said that when she had eaten her Christmas dinner she wanted to put up her feet and fall asleep by the fire and *no one* was to say the word "ironing" to her!

Mrs Larkin said that *The Sound of Music* was on television and that she watched it every year and she would like to do so again.

"Christmas time is all stress!" said Sam, lying down on the sofa. "I shall stay cool."

"You better miss Christmas dinner, then,"

said Mrs Larkin. "It might be too stressful for you."

But Sam sat up at this and said he thought he could just about cope with Christmas dinner.

Mr and Mrs Salkey said they were going to church in the morning and then they were going to walk up Crocus Street and show Winston all the lights on the Christmas trees because this was Winston's very first Christmas.

Lily and Shanta said they were going to play with the toys that Father Christmas brought them. All day!

"What about Christmas dinner?" asked Miranda-Gran. "Mrs Salkey is going to cook us a special Jamaican Christmas dinner." Lily and Shanta said they would stop for that.

But Miranda-Gran didn't get her afternoon

sleep by the fire, and Mrs Larkin didn't watch *The Sound of Music* and Shanta and Lily didn't play with their Christmas presents all day and Sam "stayed cool", but it wasn't quite the sort of "cool" he had in mind.

This is what happened.

When Shanta woke up on Christmas Day morning, her room seemed to be lit by a strange white light. Shanta saw that the sock she'd left out for Father Christmas was now bulging nicely and she sat up and reached down to the bottom of the bed for it. As she did so, she glanced out of the window. What she saw gave her an awful fright!

Clutching her Christmas sock, Shanta ran into her parents' bedroom. "There's something wrong with my eyes!" cried Shanta, jumping on to the bed and hiding her face in the eiderdown. "Everything's gone white! All the colours have gone out of the world!"

Mr Salkey sat up in bed, reached for his orange velvet cap and looked out of the window.

"Honey-bee," said Mr Salkey, "what colour is my cap?"

Shanta lifted her face out of the eiderdown and said, "Orange!"

"There's nothing wrong with those eyes of yours," said her dad. "You just haven't seen English snow before."

Then Mrs Salkey got out of bed and took Shanta to the window.

"It's like the icing sugar of the sky!" said Mrs Salkey. "It's like crumbs of fresh bread!"

Shanta looked even more surprised. "Icing sugar? Bread crumbs? Can you eat that snow-stuff?"

"No," said Mrs Salkey, "but you can have a whole snowball-full of fun with it!"

All morning it snowed and it snowed and it snowed. A few cars slithered up and down Crocus Street. Lily and Sam's dad came to call with snow on his hat and snow on his shoes and snow on the Christmas parcels he'd brought for them.

Mr and Mrs Salkey went to church in a flaky snowstorm and they showed Winston the Christmas tree lights. When they came in they said, "It's getting very deep."

Shanta and Lily played with their Christmas presents and every so often they ran to the window to see how the snow was doing.

"Spoons and scoops of icing sugar!" said Shanta.

"Loaves and loaves of breadcrumbs!" said Lily.

From upstairs in the Salkey's flat came wonderful warm smells and after a while Mr Salkey appeared at the top of the stairs with a sprig of holly in his cap and said, "Christmas dinner is ready for all you good people."

They had pumpkin soup and then Mrs Salkey brought in a great bowl of her special Jamaican dish.

"It's got all sorts of surprises in it," said Lily when she was given her plate. And it had. There were black-eyed beans and spicy chicken pieces. There were slivers of fish hiding in the rice. There were okra pods and carrots and slices of fried bananas.

"Brill!" said Sam.

"Yummy!" said Mrs Larkin.

"Happy Christmas!" said Miranda-Gran.

After the Christmas pudding (with Jamaican rum for the grown-ups) and after the crackers and hats (which Mrs Larkin had brought) and when all the dishes were done, they looked out of the window at Crocus Street covered in snow. They saw lots of families walking down the street, carrying trays. A few people had wooden boxes with a rope fixed like a handle at one end.

"Where are they all going?" asked Lily, "and why are they taking their trays?"

"I know," said Miranda-Gran. "They're going sledging in the park."

"Can we go? Can we go? Can we go?" Shanta and Lily cried at once.

And Sam said, "Yes. Sledging is cool."

"Particularly on the bottom," said Miranda-Gran.

Then all the grown-ups looked at each other and Mrs Larkin said, "I've got a tray that would make a very good sledge," and

Mr Salkey said, "We've got a fruit box. I could easily make a handle for it."

And very soon they all had their hats and coats and scarves and gloves and boots on and they were out in Crocus Street with all the other families, heading for the park.

It was very nice being out in the street. Everyone called out, "Happy Christmas!" and Lily and Shanta saw lots of their friends from nursery school. (Shanta liked nursery school now.) Everyone was wearing bright woolly hats and scarves and gloves. They were as brightly wrapped up as Christmas parcels!

The park was very good for sledging because it had low slopes and high slopes. Sam used the tray because he was old enough to go down the big slope by himself. Mr Salkey put Shanta and Lily together on the wooden-box sledge and pulled them down it. After a while they could both go by themselves, but first Lily, then Shanta, fell off into the snow.

"You're both snowy-glowy!" said Miranda-Gran after about an hour. And it was true. Lily's mittens dripped with snow but her cheeks glowed like apples.

Then Mr Salkey sat on the box-sledge and held Winston in his arms and went down the small slope very, very gently. Winston waved his arms in the air and crowed with pleasure. He tried to eat some snow but it was so cold he spat it out again.

Everything in the park looked very different covered in snow. The roundabout vanished under it. The swings each had a little cushion of snow on their seats and all the branches of the trees were topped with a finger of icing sugar.

Sam and Mr Salkey showed Lily and

Shanta how to make snowballs and then they had a snowball fight and got very wet indeed.

Soon it grew dark and everyone left the park tired but happy. Lily and Shanta were so tired that Mr Salkey said he would pull them home on the sledge. Mrs Salkey carried Winston on her back and he fell fast asleep.

When they had hung all their wet clothes up to dry and Mrs Larkin had lit the fire and drawn the curtains, Miranda-Gran made some hot chocolate. "It's too late for my afternoon nap," she said.

"And it's too late for *The Sound of Music*," said Mrs Larkin.

"Well, now," said Mr Salkey, "I suppose we better have a game of something. I don't suppose Father Christmas brought you girls any games we could play, did he?"

"He did! He did!" cried Lily and Shanta and they rushed off to fetch them. Lily had Ludo and Shanta had Snakes and Ladders and there was just time for one game of each.

"Do you know what was my best present?" Shanta asked Lily at bedtime.

"No. What?" asked Lily.

"Snow!" said Shanta.

And that was Christmas Day in Crocus Street.

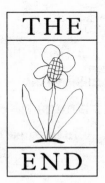

THE

END